Lover Boy
Juanito el Cariñoso

a Bilingual Counting Book

written by **Lee Merrill Byrd**

illustrations by **Francisco Delgado**

Oh, Johnny!
He's always dishing out kisses. Look!

¡Ay Juanito!
Siempre repartiendo besos. ¡Mira!

ONE little tiny one
for his big sister,
who thinks she's the boss.

UNO chiquitito para
su hermana, que piensa
que es la mera mera.

TWO big ones
for his daddy, the
pitcher whose arm
never quits.

DOS

grandotes para su papá, el pitcher
que nunca se cansa.

TRES bien cariñosos

para su mamá,
que descansa en el sofá.

FOUR served up with hugs for Mari, his teacher.

CUATRO besos con abrazos para Mari, su maestra.

FIVE
he sends
to Birdie in
the mail.

CINCO
se los manda
a Birdie
por correo.

SIX he blows to Patty
who cuts his hair.

SEIS los tira al viento para Patty
que le corta el cabello.

SEVEN
he dreams
of for Beatriz,
the girl who won't
kiss him back.

SIETE
sueña con
darle a Beatriz,
la niña que no le
regresa los besos.

EIGHT he plants on Stray Gray.

OCHO bien plantados para El Gato Gris.

NINE he gives
to Baby Ed.

NUEVE se los
da a Baby Ed.

¿**Acaso** se le han acabado los besos a Juanito el cariñoso?

Siempre reparte besos
y ¡a mí me
tocan DIEZ!

Lover Boy / Juanito El Cariñoso, A Bilingual Counting Book. Copyright © 2006 by Lee Merrill Byrd.
Illustrations copyright © 2006 by Francisco Delgado.
Translation by David Dorado Romo copyright © 2006 by Cinco Puntos Press.

FIRST EDITION
10 9 8 7 6 5 4 3 2 1

Library of Congress Cataloging-in-Publication Data

Byrd, Lee Merrill.
  Lover boy » Juanito el cariñoso / by Lee Merrill Byrd ; illustrated by Francisco Delgado.— 1st ed.
      p. cm.
  Summary: Little Johnny loves to dish out kisses, and he counts them in both English and Spanish.
  ISBN 0-938317-38-5
  [1. Kissing—Fiction. 2. Spanish language materials—Bilingual. 3. Counting.] I. Title: Juanito el cariñoso. II.
Delgado, Francisco, 1974- ill. III. Title.
  PZ73.B95 2005
  [E]--dc22
                            2005013982

For Johnny Andrew and Pedro,
Hannah, Silly Lolly, Baby Ed,
Birdie and Santiago.

Translation by David Dorado Romo, edited by Luis Humberto Crosthwaite.

Thanks to Sharon Franco for her eye on the text, as always.

Book and cover design by JB Bryan of La Alameda Press.

HFIFX   + SP
E
BYRD

BYRD, LEE MERRILL.
    LOVER BOY = JUANITO EL
CARIÑOSO
FIFTH WARD
05/07